The Native American Flute

Understanding the Gift

To
OUR FRIENDS AT
DESERT FOOTHILLS LIBRARY

John Vames

Copyright © 2003 **John Vames and Molly Moon Arts & Publishing:**
8513 East Mulberry Street, Scottsdale, AZ 85251
2nd Edition, 2005, compiled & edited by Sherry Fields-Vames,
Original graphic design by Leonard Potter of Leonardo Designs
Front cover photography and design by Patricia L.A. Moore

ISBN 0-9740486-2-3

Acknowledgements

I want to thank all my students at Scottsdale Community College for their continued interest, input and suggestions. My special thanks to our graphic designer Leonard Potter of Leonardo Designs, and our sound engineer Randall Huot for their expertise and patience in putting this project together. Also, a special thanks to Don DeLong for his help. Last but not least, I would like to thank my wife Sherry for her untold hours of reading and editing this material. Without her dedication this book would not have been possible.

Preface

Of the many gifts our Native ancestors have given us, the Native American Flute is indeed a favorite.

In addition to being visually beautiful, it has a haunting sound that many profess has the power to soothe and heal. Once heard most people experience a strong desire to play it themselves. What is so encouraging is that almost anyone regardless of prior musical experience can learn to play in a short time. Unlike piano and guitar that require years of study, the magic of this instrument asks only that the player breathe into it and cover the tone holes correctly. With just a little bit of practice beautiful sounds can emerge and we are the creators. Such is the gift of *this* Music.

For over thirty years I have been a professional woodwind player and educator. Like you, I too have been strongly attracted to this magical instrument. My love for it has gone far beyond learning to play and in the past years I have helped hundreds of people get started on musical journeys of their own. It is with great pleasure that I share this.

The information I have presented in this text is taken from my classes and is designed for your success. If you can spend some quiet time each day with your flute I promise that in a short while you will develop the tools necessary to play the songs in your heart.

Thank you for your interest in this wonderful gift from our ancestors and know that soon it will be you who share the magic. Please do so, for it is a gift meant to pass on. Our world will be a better place.

Peace,

John Vames

Table of Contents:

Part II   Songs

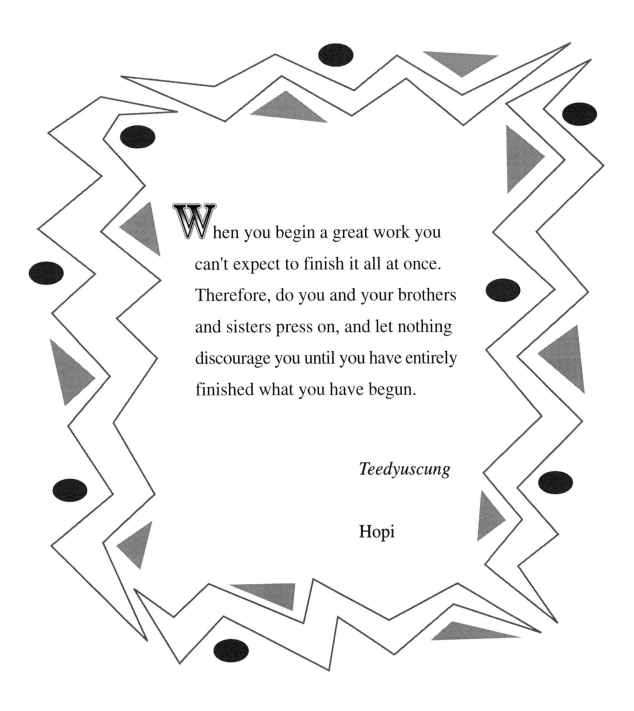

When you begin a great work you can't expect to finish it all at once. Therefore, do you and your brothers and sisters press on, and let nothing discourage you until you have entirely finished what you have begun.

Teedyuscung

Hopi

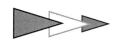 # Introduction
How to Use this Book
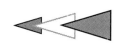

Most people are very enthusiastic when they begin a project, as I'm sure you are in learning to play your flute. The learning process can be fun for the entire duration if you get organized and have a plan. Three important parts of this plan should be:

1. Find time or make time to play your flute every day especially for the first month after you start playing.

2. At the end of every session you should be able to do something you could not do when you started.

3. Put together a *"Learning Kit"*. This should include your flute, this Book, a portable CD player and a notebook and pencil to jot down some instruction in your own words. Also, a mirror to check your hand position and embouchure. Everything can be kept in a flat box, on a desk, table, TV, or any place you may find in your home. The point being that everything you need to learn to play will be in one place and easily accessible.

   On all of the examples on the accompanying CD I have used an A minor flute.

***Put these suggestions into use and you will
succeed and have a good time doing it.***

This Book is organized into Six lessons. Each Lesson has several parts which should be practiced separately until mastered before going on to the next. *The one exception is Lesson One.* Here you should work on finger control, breath control, and an initial exploration of the six basic notes on your flute. Spend ALL your playing time on this phase for at least one week and your flute progress will be fast and enjoyable!

From lesson one onward, first read the text, study pictures and diagrams, and listen to the CD tracks that demonstrate what you read. Then pick up your flute and play the lesson over and over again until it is yours; until your understanding is automatic and you don't have to think about it anymore. This may take days and in some instances even weeks. Don't allow yourself to become discouraged or frustrated. Learn to enjoy the process and you will be rewarded with daily progress.

Habit is a miraculous thing. In the beginning it takes conscious effort on your part to do what we have been talking about. Keep on though and remember that in a short time the habit of daily practice and the learning of new techniques will light your way.

Good luck on your journey
and may the force be with you!

A feather is a sacred universal symbol of flight within the spirit world and serves as messenger to the Great Spirit. When feathers are fanned in a circle they are communicating a message to the Sun and The Creator.

Finger Control

Breath Control

Knowing Your Flute

Embouchure

Basic Notes

Tonguing and Slurring

Notes

Finger Control

The first step in learning to play the Native American Flute is to understand and practice *finger control*. Finger control means covering and uncovering the tone holes with *precision.*

We use the first, second and third fingers on each hand to cover the six holes of the flute.

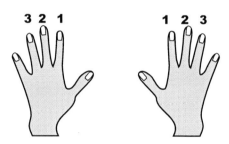

Before picking up your flute, hold your hands in front of you and tap the first, second and third fingers against the thumbs, as if you were playing finger cymbals. Make sure the tips of your fingers are flattened as you come into contact with the thumb.

Correct way

Incorrect way

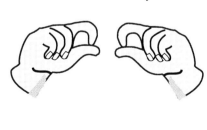

Pad

3

Try working both hands at the same time saying "one, two, three" as you tap against your thumbs over and over again. The fingers should hinge at the third joint that is the knuckle. By doing this for five minutes at the beginning of each playing and practice session you will:

◇ Learn correct finger action
◇ Feel the pad behind each finger tip
◇ Learn to act with a regular rhythm

Now pick up your flute with your left hand, holes facing upward. Count the tone holes from top to bottom while looking at them.

Next, turn your flute so the holes face away from you and with the thumbs in back for support, place your fingers on the tone holes, *left hand on top, right hand on the bottom. (Fig. 1)*

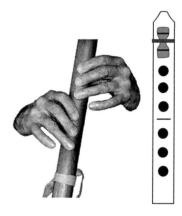

With *both* hands on the flute, practice opening and closing the holes using the same action you used when "playing" finger cymbals.

(Fig. 1)   6 holes covered

Note: Your first attempt to produce a sound may result in a squeak or squeal. The reasons for this usually are: *First*, you may not be covering the tone holes completely with the pad behind the fingertip pressed firmly. *Second*, you could be blowing too hard and doing so can cause the tone to jump to a high undesirable pitch. Remember that the Native American Flute is a peaceful instrument. It simply requires a smooth, gentle, steady stream of air to produce its magic.

 # Breath Control

Our discussion of breath control will deal with:

- Correct technique for inhaling and exhaling while playing your flute
- Embouchure: the Lip/Flute Connection
- The use of the tongue to give tones a clean, definite start.

First, follow your normal breathing for a few minutes. Cold air hits your nostrils as you inhale. Can you feel it? The cold air then warms up on its way to your throat and we hardly feel it when it gets there.

Next, become aware that your abdomen pokes out a little when you *inhale* and then returns to normal when you *exhale*. As a matter of fact, you will feel a slight expansion all around your waist as you inhale.

This expansion of the abdomen and waist is caused by a downward movement of your *diaphragm*. The diaphragm is the second strongest muscle in the body. It separates the chest cavity from the abdominal cavity and is responsible for filling and emptying the lungs with air. It is an involuntary muscle that cannot be consciously controlled like opening and closing your fist. It will take time, but with practice you can become aware of this movement and use this awareness to control the flow of air when playing.

(Fig. 2) shows the lungs, illustrating how the diaphragm moves when you inhale and exhale. Study the path of air as you breathe in and out and see if you feel the movement of this muscle.

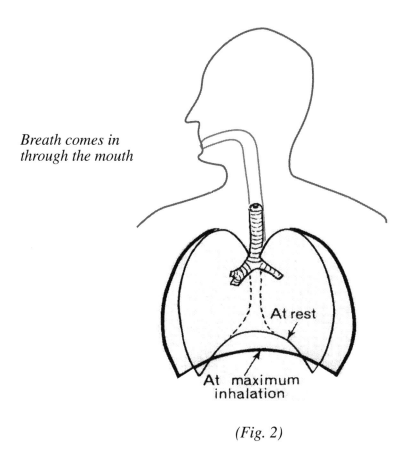

Breath comes in through the mouth

At rest

At maximum inhalation

(Fig. 2)

In normal breathing, inhaling and exhaling are about equal in duration. To play a wind instrument however, you need to take in a lot of air quickly and learn to release it over a long period of time. To accomplish this you will need to breathe in *through the mouth and not the nose.*

Developing Correct Breath Control:

Track #1

Look at *fig. 2*. Concentrate on breathing in and out through your mouth. You should feel cold air hitting your throat. As you practice the following exercise, **do not let your shoulders rise up.** The movement should be in the abdomen and the waist only.

Count to four at a steady pace: 1, 2, 3, 4.

Inhale at the Same pace, through your mouth for four counts 1, 2, 3, 4.

Exhale using a hissing sound for 8 to 12 counts.

Count	Inhale	Exhale (hiss)
1 2 3 4	1 2 3 4	1 2 3 4 5 6 7 8

Note: Not only will this exercise help you develop breath control for your flute it will also help you relax and relieve stress. Oxygen is a wonderful friend to the human body. If you already practice yoga or meditations you'll have a head start. Enjoy this practice routine and do it often. *Now, turn off Track #1 and practice it five times!*

Remember, it is your breath that powers this instrument and makes the wood come alive.

Knowing Your Flute

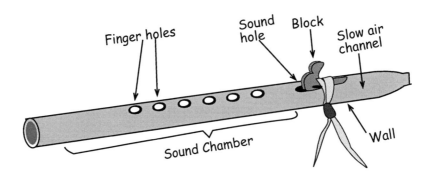

The *fetish* or block as it is sometimes called is adjustable. If you slide the stop too far forward the lower notes will sound windy; too far back and the higher notes will fade. If the fetish is knocked out of adjustment, slide it forward or backwards (sometimes sideways) until all the notes sound clear and uniform.

Keep the air channel beneath the fetish base clean and free of particles. Any particles in the air channel will disrupt the air flow and your flute will not play properly.

Leather Strapping

The leather strap secures the fetish to the flute and makes the fetish adjustable. The strap must be tight at all times to prevent air leakage from the air channel. Air leakage will cause windy or breathy sounding notes.

Retying or Tightening the Leather Strap

When retying or tightening the leather strap make sure it is pulled very tightly when making your first knot. If the strap breaks, any leather shop can provide new leather. A strip of cloth works as well.

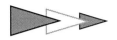 

Embouchure is a French word meaning how the lips engage and hold the instrument you are playing. I like to call it simply the *lip/flute connection.*

To begin, open your mouth by dropping the jaw just a little. Stretch the lower lip slightly against the lower teeth. (*Fig. 3*)

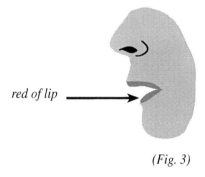

red of lip ——————→

(Fig. 3)

Now, rest the flute on the *red of the lip* and close the mouth to form a seal. *(Fig. 4)*

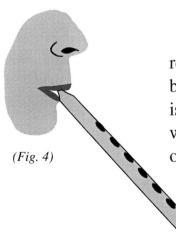

(Fig. 4)

Note: The flute does not go into your mouth. It rests on the cushion made by the lower lip backed by the lower teeth. (*Fig. 4*) From this position it is easy to take air through the corners of the mouth without moving the flute from its resting place on the lower lip. Try it!

You are Now ready to begin playing your first notes...

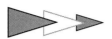 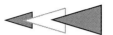

Track # 2

You will need to work closely with the CD. In each example black circles indicate holes covered, white circles are opened.

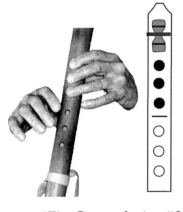

(Fig. 5)   playing "3"

Cover holes 1, 2 and 3 with the first, second and third fingers of the left hand. *The concept of these 3 holes covered will be referred to as "3" (Fig. 5).*

The right hand thumb will be under the flute with the three fingers of the right hand poised about one inch above holes 4, 5, and 6. Visualize your diaphragm as you take your breath. Blow into the flute with a smooth, gentle stream of air much like you would blow on a spoon of hot soup to cool it.

Make sure you can feel all the rim of each hole under each finger, but do not squeeze.

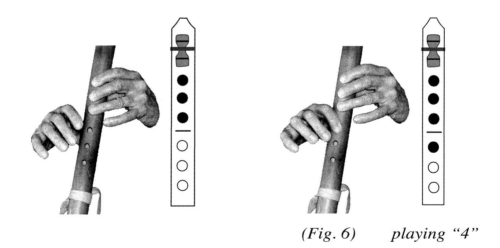

(Fig. 6)   playing "4"

Next, start with " 3" and with the same breath, play "4" (Fig. 6)

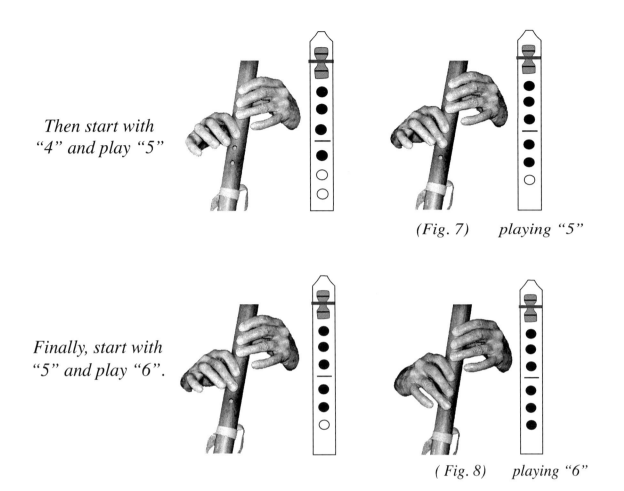

Then start with "4" and play "5"

(Fig. 7)   playing "5"

Finally, start with "5" and play "6".

(Fig. 8)   playing "6"

You have now played four of the six basic notes. *(Fig. 9)*

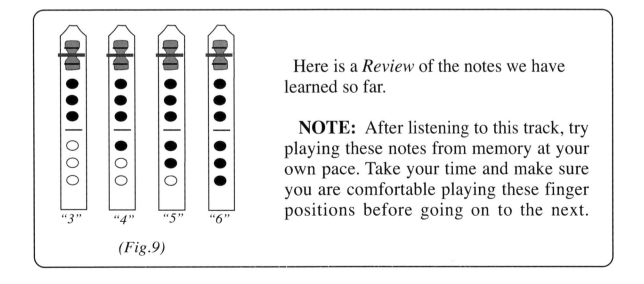

"3"   "4"   "5"   "6"

(Fig.9)

Here is a *Review* of the notes we have learned so far.

NOTE: After listening to this track, try playing these notes from memory at your own pace. Take your time and make sure you are comfortable playing these finger positions before going on to the next.

We will now look at the remaining two notes of the basic scale:

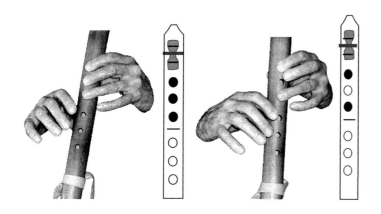

As before start with " 3" covered. Play and while holding the note, LIFT the second finger. *(Fig. 10)* . This finger position is written as. " $\frac{1}{3}$ "

Track #3

(Fig. 10)   playing " $\frac{1}{3}$ "

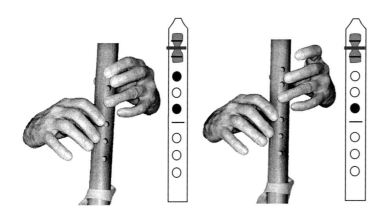

Next, start with holes 1 and 3 covered and lift the 1st finger of the left hand as you blow *(Fig. 11)* This finger position is called "circle 3" and will be written as "③" This is the highest note we will learn at this time.

(Fig. 11)   playing "③"

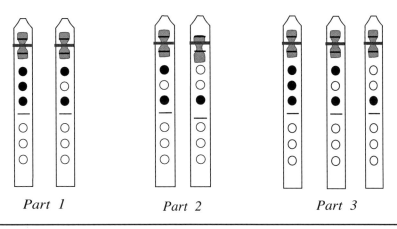

Developing technique for fingers of the left hand.

Start with "3" with your left hand. Lift the second finger as you keep the air flow going. (*Part I*). *Next* start with the first and third finger down and lift the first finger (*Part 2*). *Finally*, play "3" then "$\frac{1}{3}$" and "③"(*Part 3*) .

Part 1   *Part 2*   *Part 3*

(Fig. 12)

NOTE: Notice in playing all six basic notes the third hole from the top always remains *covered*.

Tonguing and Slurring *Track #4*

To help our breath give a note a clean, definite start, we use a technique called *tonguing*. The tip of the tongue is placed in contact with the roof of the mouth just behind the upper teeth. Take a breath and as you exhale think of the tongue as a valve that releases the air when you whisper "doo". This gives the note a gentle start and leads to a smooth line when you tongue a series of notes. (A vigorous attack with the tongue produces an effect called *chirping*. Use this sound with discretion.)

There is also a second possibility you may choose when playing a series of notes; Tongue the first note only, keep the air flow going and just move your fingers. The sound created is called *slurring*. In playing a melody some notes are tongued and some notes are slurred. It's up to you. The only time you must tongue is when you repeat the *same* note two or three times. Some notes in the next melody are slurred and some tongued. See if you can hear the difference.

Notes

Review

Finger Control: Covering and uncovering the tone holes with *precision* will give you a "clean" sound moving from one note to another.

Breath Control: To sustain a pleasing tone inhale quickly through your mouth and exhale slowly over an extended period of time through your flute.

Embouchure: The lip/flute connection. Remember the flute does not go into your mouth but rests on the red of the lower lip.

Basic Flute notes: It is important to master the finger positions of these six basic notes: 6 5 4 3 $\frac{1}{3}$ ③ . It is the foundation for learning to play well and spontaneously.

Tonguing and Slurring: These techniques will add variety to your playing.

Congratulations. You have completed lesson 1.

"Everything an Indian does is done in a circle, and that is because the Power of the World always works in circles, and everything tries to be round…The Sky is round, and I have heard the earth is round like a ball, and so are the stars. The Wind in its greatest power, whirls. Birds make their nests in circles; for theirs is the same Religion as ours…Even the Seasons form a circle in their changing, and always come back again to where they were. The life of man is a circle from childhood to childhood, and so it is with everything where power moves."

-Black Elk, Ogala

Lesson 2

The Native American Scale

Creating Your Own Melodies
Using rhythm patterns to create songs

A Traditional Native Love Song
"Lakota Courting Song"

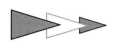 

The Native American Scale is also called the Minor Pentatonic Scale

To play your flute well you must play this scale from low to high, and high to low many times until it becomes automatic.

Track #5

Here is how the scale looks in pictures and finger diagrams. *(Fig.15-20)*
You are already familiar with these notes.

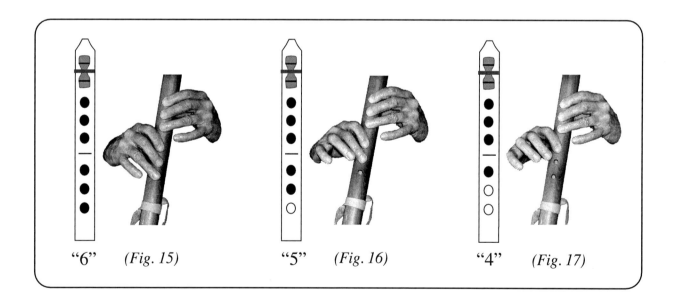

"6"   *(Fig. 15)*   "5"   *(Fig. 16)*   "4"   *(Fig. 17)*

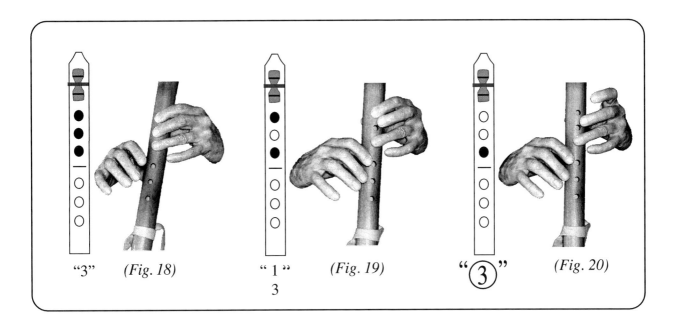

"3" *(Fig. 18)*   " 1 " *(Fig. 19)*   "③" *(Fig. 20)*
                          3

Practice Tips

Play this scale *many* times! Look into a mirror to see that the tone holes are completely covered.

You can also try playing it with your eyes closed. This will help you get the feel of each hole under your fingers. Listen carefully to the sound of each note in relation to its neighbors. Musicians call this *aural perception.*

Again, *it is very important to be able to play this scale correctly and fluently.*
It is the basic foundation for mastering all that follows.

Before going on to the next concept please review.

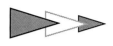 # Creating Your Own Melodies

Using "rhythm patterns" to make up songs  *Track #6*

> Before listening to track # 6 read through the following text and become familiar with the terms you will hear me using.

For the purpose of our understanding, I will be describing a" rhythm pattern" as a combination of short or long tones, illustrated by symbol ⌣ = short — = long

For example, a "⌣, — " means you will play one tone of *short* duration followed by one tone of *long* duration.

Further rhythm patterns for our study are as follows:

> *Short, short, long* = ⌣⌣ —
> 2 short tones followed by one long
>
> *Short, short, short, long* = ⌣ ⌣ ⌣ —
> 3 short tones followed by one long
>
> *Short, short, short, short, long* = ⌣ ⌣ ⌣ ⌣ —
> 4 short tones followed by one long

20

Playing Rhythm Patterns

Play all the "short, long" rhythm patterns from *track # 6* until they are memorized. *Next*, choose one pattern you like and play any note or combination of notes from the Native American Scale in any order that pleases you.

For example, on pattern *"short, short, short, long"*. You might play 3, 3, 4, 3, or 6, 3, 4, 5.

Remember that the rhythm pattern remains the same. Only the notes you play will be different.

A good analogy is to think of a Kaleidoscope with six pieces of colored glass. Every time I turn it a little a new picture emerges. No two exactly alike. In the same manner, every time you play a consistent rhythm pattern using a different series of notes, you will have created a "new" song.

 Track #7 demonstrates further variations and patterns for creating songs using these rhythm symbols as applied to the following:

— ◡ — ◡ — ◡ —

Jack and Jill went up the hill

It is now time to introduce your first Native American Song....

As legend has it ...

A young brave on a horse was riding and noticed a woodpecker on a branch. He had a feeling that the woodpecker was trying to tell him something. He got off his horse and walked over to the branch where the bird sat.

When he got there, the woodpecker flew away, but the young brave noticed the bird had pecked five holes. He broke the branch off the tree, and as he stood there holding it, the wind rushed through it and the wood made a sound. He took this magical stick to a medicine man and asked him what this meant.

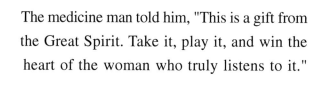

The medicine man told him, "This is a gift from the Great Spirit. Take it, play it, and win the heart of the woman who truly listens to it."

From that day, many of the courting flutes have their head in the shape of a woodpecker.

Lakota Courting Song

Using the illustration of finger diagrams and the rhythm symbols indicated above each flute you will know what notes to play and what duration they will be. *Go to*  *Track #8, **listen** and then play. (Each line is played twice).*

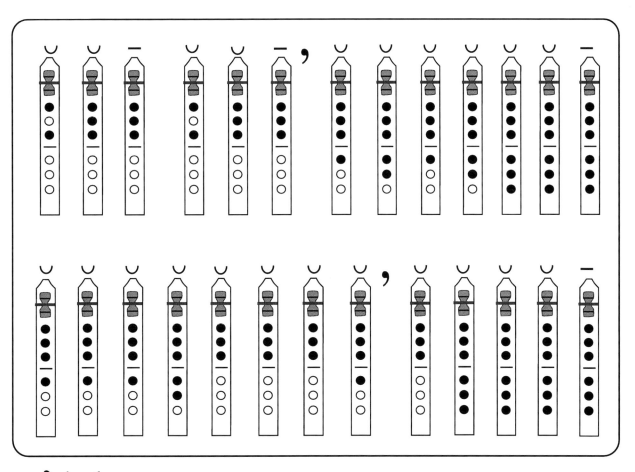

🎵 = breath

Notes

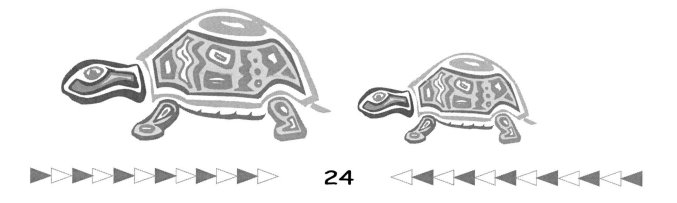

Ornaments Part I

Grace Notes and Variations
Trills, Mordents and the "Ending Pop"

Application of Ornaments

"Lakota Courting Song"

Duration Part I
Reading Duration Values

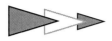 

Ornaments are what we use to embellish or decorate the basic melodies we play. The most common and most often heard of these is the *grace note*. It is a very short note that is literally *crushed* into the note you really intended to play.

Playing Grace Notes

To play a grace note, start with an open hole above the note you intend to play. *For instance:* You want to play 4, so you start with 3 and then drop your finger down very fast on 4. *Sounds like this:* 🔘 *Track # 9*

We have played a grace note to each of the main notes of the Native American scale. *Next*, listen as I play each one of the following three times, and then you play each one three times.

Repeat track # 9 until you feel comfortable with the concept.

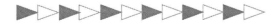 

Variations on grace notes: 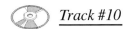 <u>*Track #10*</u>

You can hold a note and then at some point before you end it, lift your finger and put it back quickly. I call this a *flip*.

Another variation is to do a *flip* up and down at the beginning of a phrase. This is called a *mordent*. If this action is done more than three times the sound would be called a *trill*. A trill is a rapid alternation between the main note and the next highest note on your flute.

> *Treat these variations on grace notes the same way you did the basic grace note. They should be practiced and played on each note of the scale so you will be able to insert them at any time you like when you play.*

Another ornament I hear often occurs at the end of a solo, although it may also occur at various places during a solo. I am referring to the *ending pop*. At the end of your last note, increase your air pressure suddenly and say the word "What" as you release the fingers at the same time. (On some flutes, keeping all holes closed and gradually increasing the air pressure produces a note an octave higher. This effect is called *overblowing*.)

Applying Ornaments to Lakota Courting Song <u>*Track #11*</u>

On this *track*, I will play Lakota Courting Song. First without, and then with ornamentation. Listen as many times as necessary then copy what you hear on your flute. The purpose is not to do it my way, but rather to learn the technique so you can do it your way.

Practice this track everyday for at least one week. In time you will begin to ornament melodies automatically.

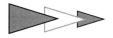 Duration: Part I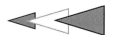

In Lesson 2 we learned how to use basic notation for reading a rhythm pattern. The symbols of short (⌣) and long (—) helped us understand the approximate length of time a tone should be held. We will now take a closer look at *Duration* and will learn to recognize the *exact* length of time a tone will be held.

We will approach this important subject with a series of easy to understand statements, numbered 1-10. Try to understand each one before going on to the next and before you turn on CD *Track #12*.

1. Music is an *art form* in time.
2. We measure the passage of time with *pulses* or *beats*.
3. We organize these beats into units of three, four, or six beats.
4. The most common unit of time is four beats.
5. *Fig. 21* shows a time line. It is divided into four small units by vertical lines called *bar lines*.

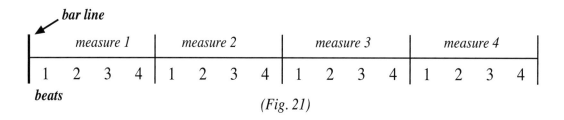

(Fig. 21)

6. The space between each bar line is one measure of musical time.

7. The numbers indicate that each measure lasts for four beats.

8.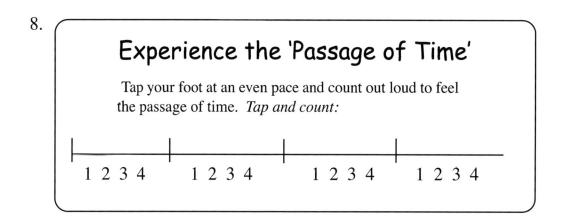

9. Musicians use symbols called *notes* which indicate the number of beats a tone should be held. *Here are the first three note symbols you need to learn.*

⚬ is a whole note worth four beats

♩ is a half note worth two beats

♩ is a quarter note worth one beat

10. Using our *time line* we will now place a *whole* note in each measure. *(Fig.22)*. The number above each note indicates the finger position used on the CD. *Each note will get four beats.* *Track #12*

11.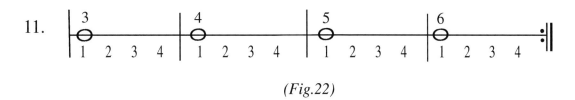

(Fig.22)

Notice the *repeat sign* at the end of the measure. It means to play the line again.

Reading Duration Values: *Half Notes and Quarter Notes* 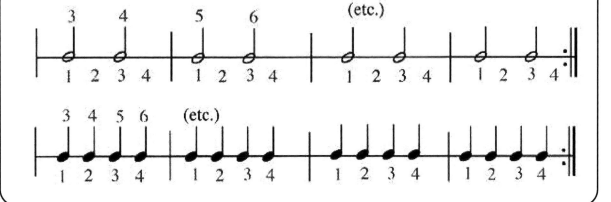 *Track #13*

*This exercise has 2 parts; **First**, count out loud and clap your hands for the duration of each note.* You need to keep your hands together for the duration of each note value. This represents sustaining, or holding a note on your flute. ***Next**, tap your foot and play the finger position indicated above each measure.* Remember that each bar will get four beats.

(Fig. 23)

Our next practice, (*Fig. 24*), **combines** different note values. There are three different examples: A, B, and C. *Some useful study tips for this exercise are as follows:*

1. First count out loud and clap the rhythm
2. Next, tap your foot and play the rhythm. Use "3" only.
3. Now play the notes of the *Native American/Pentatonic Scale* starting with the lowest "6", and going to the highest "③"

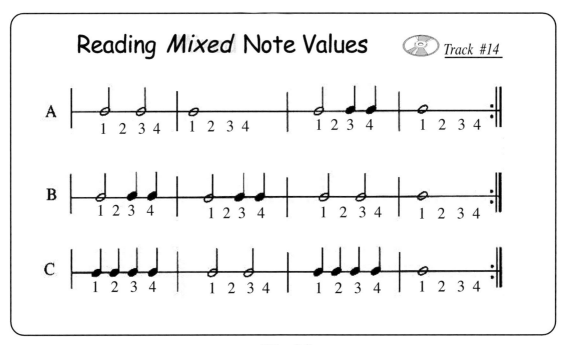

(*Fig. 24*)

When you feel confident with this go on to the next. Take your time and do not go ahead until you are comfortable with the material. You will know you are ready when you can play the exercise in a smooth flowing style without hesitation.

Before we close on Lesson 3 here is one last challenge! *(Fig.25)*

We will repeat the previous exercise, but this time, instead of playing the indicated finger positions you are now *free* to play whatever note you like from the Native American Scale, just as you did when playing short and long rhythm patterns. Like before you may repeat notes, skip notes, and move up and down. The choice is yours. The difference now is that you are reading and playing *note values* exactly as they are notated.

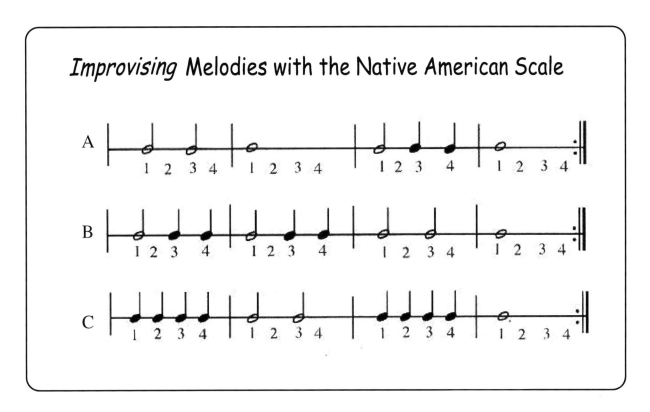

(Fig. 25)

Review

Ornaments: The grace note with its variations is the most used embellishment in flute playing. Learn to use it with all the notes on your flute.

Rhythmic Notation: The system of symbols that indicate how long a note should be sustained. In this lesson we learned three: whole note, half note, and quarter note.

Bar Lines: Vertical lines that separate notation into small units.

Measure: the amount of music between two bar lines. Musicians often refer to a measure as a bar of music.

Improvising: As used in this lesson, making up melodies based on a pre-arranged rhythm pattern and random notes of the Native American Scale.

Congratulations! You have completed lesson 3.

Ornaments Part II

Bending
Double Tonguing
Vibrato

Zuni Sunrise Song

Duration Part II

Relative Note Durations
Eighth notes
Dotted quarter and half notes
Sixteenth notes

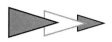 # Ornaments Part II

Here are some techniques to help you further embellish melodies.

The **bend** or **slide** is when a note seems to *glide up or down* to the next note in a smooth way. This is done by pushing a finger forward and gradually off the tone hole. Try it from a lower to a higher note.

This is called *bending up* $_4\!\!\int^3$

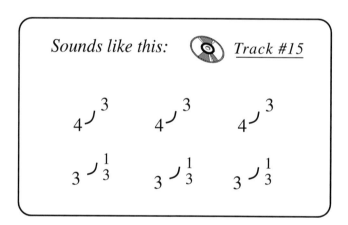

Sounds like this: Track #15

$_4\!\!\int^3$ $_4\!\!\int^3$ $_4\!\!\int^3$

$_3\!\!\int_3^1$ $_3\!\!\int_3^1$ $_3\!\!\int_3^1$

Continue with the following: $_6\!\!\int^5$ $_5\!\!\int^4$ $_{1\atop3}\!\!\int^③$

Bending down is more difficult. For now I suggest you just let the sound drop by gradually slowing down the air flow until it stops. *Try it on each note of the scale.*

Flutter Tongue

   This is an ornament that I would use sparingly. If you can make the sound of the Spanish "R" with the tip of your tongue that's it! If you can not, try it this way; Start a tone, 3 is a good one, and begin to raise a relaxed tongue toward the roof of your mouth. As it reaches the air stream it will begin to vibrate creating the sound we call flutter tongue.

Double Tonguing:

   This is accomplished with a two-part tongue action. When you say "Tu" the tip of your tongue touches the roof of your mouth behind the upper teeth. When you say "Ku" your tongue arches and touches the roof of your mouth near the middle. Try it...Say "Tu - Ku - Tu - Ku" slowly. Gradually speed up the action until it is moving twice as fast as you can possibly single tongue (Tu - Ku - Tu - Ku, etc).

Vibrato

   This is the wave in the sound of the flute that gives it warmth and helps with emotional expression.

> ***Note:*** Work closely with the CD. Vibrato will take time to master but is well worth the effort. The following instructions (1-9) will be demonstrated on   *Track #16*

1. Expel your breath with a sigh. Be aware that the diaphragm is controlling the action. (Your abdomen will move out and back in.)
   Sigh into your flute.

2. As you sigh the air flow slows down and the tone dies away.

3. After a few trials with this, experiment with bringing the tone back up with a push of air before it dies. It might look like this in (*Fig. 26*)

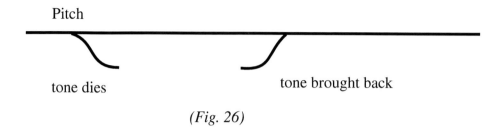

(Fig. 26)

4. Starting with the top three holes covered with the left hand practice *one, two, three and four dips per beat.*

5. Start with a very slow beat and gradually increase the speed.

6. At this stage you are not producing a useable vibrato. It will not sound like the finished product but rather like a rough version of the dip and rise of a siren.

7. You should practice the wave motion of Vibrato on all six notes of the Native American scale. *Some are easier to dip than others.*

8. The wave effect should start with the correct pitch, dip down and come back up. (*Fig. 27*)

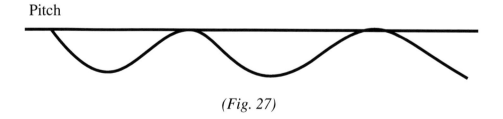

(Fig. 27)

9. The final goal is to make vibrato become part of your sound as demonstrated on the CD.

Zuni Sunrise Song

Here is a second Native American Song. I have chosen what is perhaps the best known song in the Southwest. "Zuni Sunrise". It is played or sung at sunrise to welcome back the sun and thank it for shining on earth for another day.

 *Track #17*

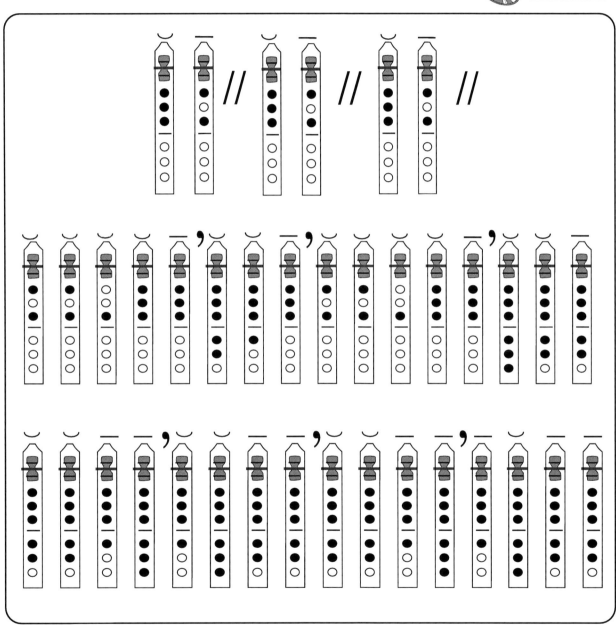

, = breath   **//** = pause

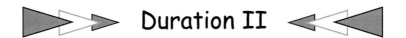
Relative Note Duration

1. Notes are of relative duration, one to the other

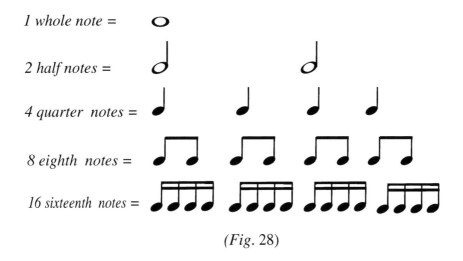

(*Fig.* 28)

 Track #18

2. We have already studied the first three note values in (*Fig.* 28) above. Let's look at the fourth one: Eighth notes.

3. Notice that there are two eighth notes for every quarter note. This means they are twice as fast.

4. Saying short, short, long while looking at (*Fig.* 29) will help you get the feel of eighth notes.

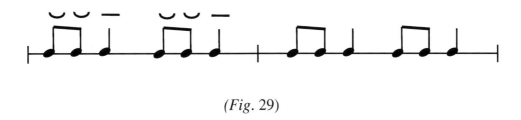

(*Fig.* 29)

5. To be more accurate look at *(Fig. 30)* count out loud as written, saying "One & two & three & four &"

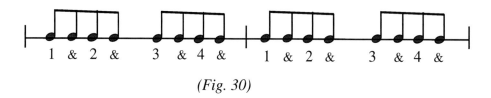

1 & 2 & 3 & 4 & 1 & 2 & 3 & 4 &

(Fig. 30)

6. *Now* tap and play on one note.

7. *Next*, play sequence 3, 4, 5, 6

8. Try it again and while still counting out loud, clap your hands in time to the beats in *(Fig. 31)*. *You are now clapping and counting Eighth notes.*

9.

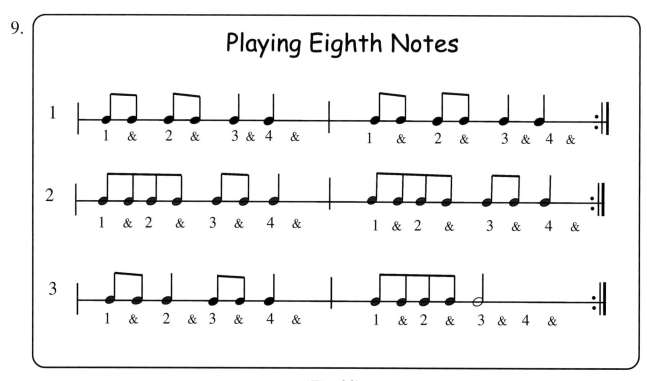

(Fig. 31)

Dotted Note Values  *Track #19*

When a "dot" is added to either a quarter note or half note, it increases that note's value by half.

A *dotted half* note gets three beats

A *dotted quarter* note gets one and a half beats

In *(Fig. 32)* are three rhythm patterns mixing the duration values we have covered. Most important in practicing this is *to Take Your Time.*

Each exercise is four measures long. Play each one twice in the following order:

First play on "3".
Next, use 3 – 4 – 5 – 6, but not always in that order as illustrated on the CD.
Finally, use the entire scale from low to high .

(Fig. 32)

Sixteenth Notes

In closing this lesson, I would like to acquaint you with one more duration value: the sixteenth note.

The shortest note value found in most printed music you will be playing is the sixteenth note. It is often found in groups of two and four like the eighth note. To distinguish it from the eighth note, however, it has a double beam.

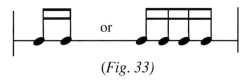

(Fig. 33)

What will suffice in terms of your general understanding at the present time is to know that as an eigth note is counted as 1 "&" 2 "&" 3 "&" 4 "&". A sixteenth note which is twice as fast as an eighth is counted in the following way:

        1 e & a / 2 e & a / etc.   Spoken, "one ee and a"

We count this way because there are four sixteenth notes to one beat. This means we must add additional syllables to our count to reflect the correct beat.

        1 e & a / 2 e & a / etc.

I demonstrate sixteenth notes on  *Track #20*

Listen Only so you may get acquainted with the sound and feel of these notes. You will know when you are ready to play sixteenth notes, and when you are you will find plenty of printed material to help you.

Congratulations on Completing Lesson 4.

Definition of *Music* among Native American Tribes:

"A ritual of communication with the Great Spirit with the singer's Life Breath; a method of settling disputes between tribes."

- Indian Sun

Reading Music

What is and has always been important is man's ability to decipher the written symbols of the day in order to communicate. That's what reading Music is about and it is now time to look at the history of the written sound in order to understand its value for us in the present.

History of Written Music

Tablature was a form of pitch designation which can be traced back to the middle ages. It designated Pitch in a general way with symbols of hand movement. It did not include any means of indicating duration.

Music at that time was all religious and vocal, sung by Monks in Monasteries. The melodies of their chants were handed down by oral tradition which meant they already knew the rhythm because it was dictated by the words. Tablature served to refresh their memories of the melody. Also, with one Monk as the leader, it kept the group together when they sang.

As music developed it left the monasteries and became secular as well as religious. It also became instrumental as well as vocal. Just as spoken language was being written down to preserve it and pass it on to future generations, so too was music.

The problem with music notation though, was that there was a need for a system to indicate both pitch (how high or low a tone sounds) and duration (how long a note is sustained).

It wasn't until the 12th century that some genius in a monastery came up with the idea of a staff to indicate pitch and note symbols to indicate duration. This invention was as important to music as the invention of the printing press was to the written word. It revolutionized the way music was composed, written, played and sung.

Today, music is written by placing the duration symbols you have been learning on a *staff* made up of five lines and four spaces. *(Fig. 34)*

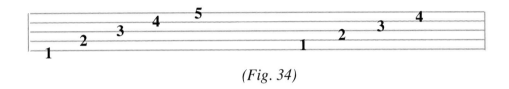

(Fig. 34)

To illustrate, let us now place our notes of the Native American scale, from low to high, left to right, on the lines and the spaces of the staff below.

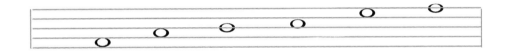

Following, are the same six notes, now with their corresponding finger diagrams relating to your flute. *(Fig. 35)*

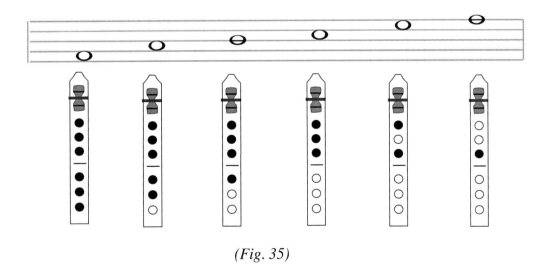

(Fig. 35)

Once you have memorized and associated each of the fingering diagrams with its designated place on the staff you are on your way to reading tablature. Here is a practice exercise to help with memorization:

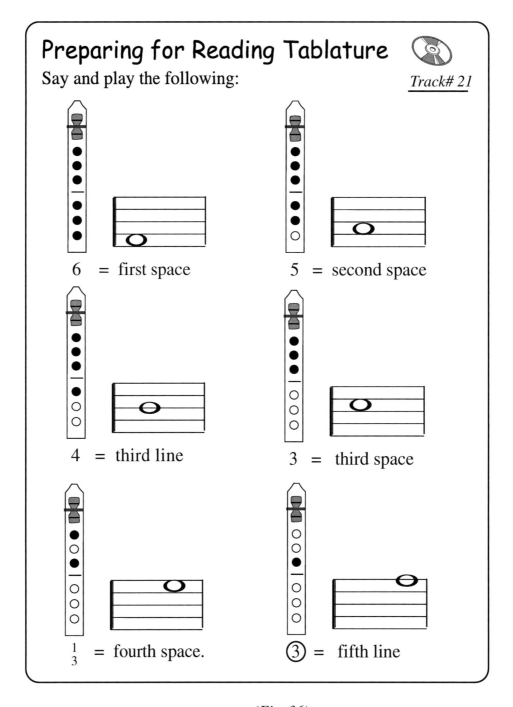

(Fig. 36)

Musicians read music by recognizing the fingering required when they see symbols placed on a staff. These are the symbols that we have learned in the lesson on *Duration*. These symbols also tell us how long to sustain them.

NOTE: *The important difference between the finger diagrams and the notes on the staff is:*

Finger diagrams indicate pitch only. That is, how high or how low the note will sound. Notes placed on the staff indicate pitch and duration. This means in addition to knowing what fingers to use, you will also know how long to sustain each note.

In the following three pages of *tablature* exercises we are concerned only with memorizing the combination of note placement on the staff with fingering for each of the notes on our flute. Move from one note to the next at your own pace. Only the bare essentials are used for these exercises: There is a *staff*, *whole note symbols* only, and *bar lines* to separate each one. Duration of each note is up to you.

Play each exercise over and over again, playing each line several times before going on to the next. *I'm sure you will be delighted as your sight reading ability develops.* When you are satisfied with your knowledge try playing the 2 traditional songs on page 53 written in Tablature.

Native American Tablature # 1

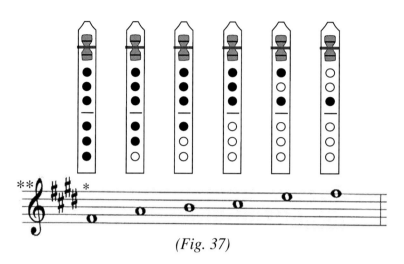

(Fig. 37)

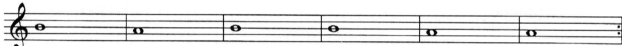

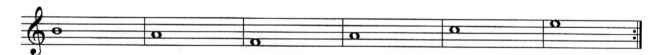

* All songs that are written in Nakai Tablature have four sharps (####) in their key signature. It is not necessary to understand the concept of key signature to learn tablature and I have omitted it from the following exercises. For details on Nakai Tablature see *The Art of The Native American Flute*, by R. C. Nakai and James DeMars

** For explanation of the *treble clef* see glossary

Tablature # 2

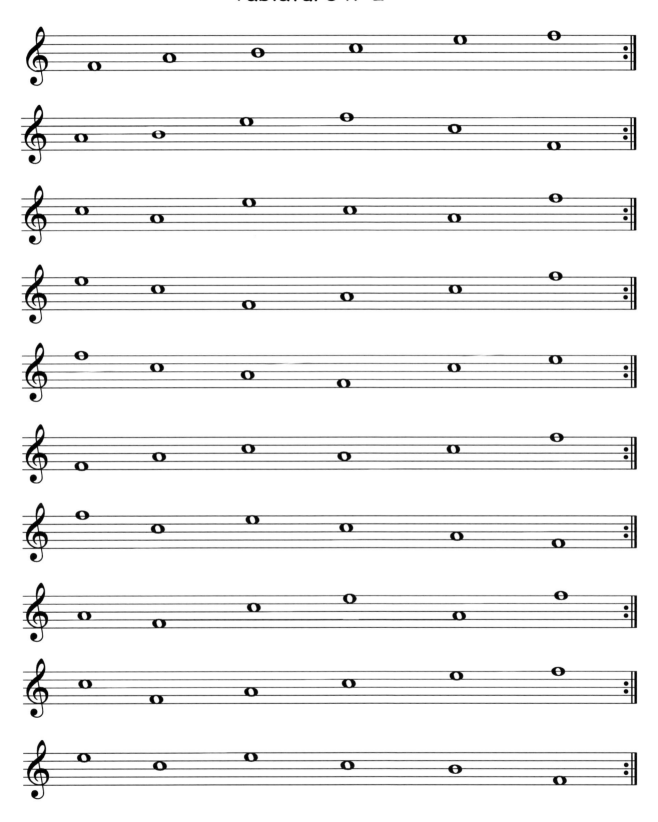

Tablature # 3

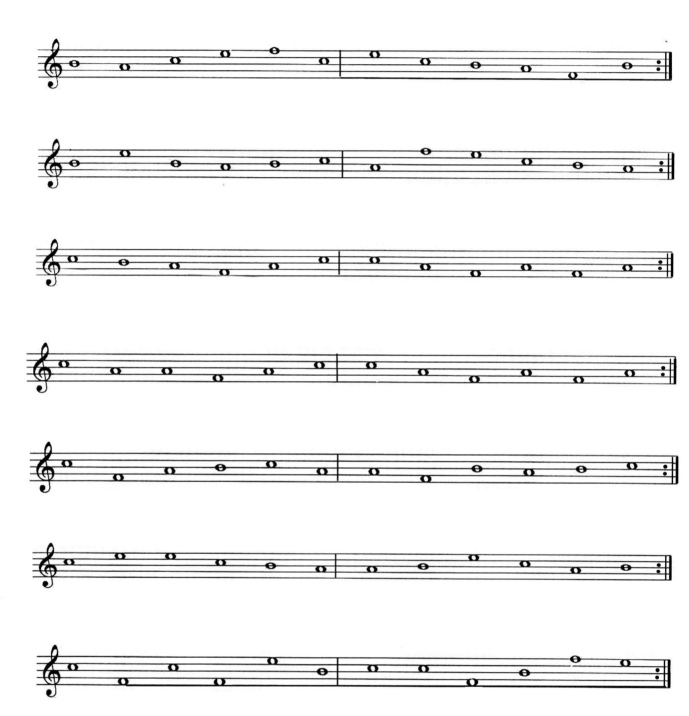

Lakota Courting Song

Track 8

Zuni Sunrise

Track 17

*The Key signature of most of the songs in this book have three sharps. I explained the reason for this in Appendix II.

53

Review

Tablature: a system of notation used to indicate the pitch of a note only. This means how high or how low a note is to sound without indication of duration nor the use of a staff.

Nakai Tablature: A system of musical notation developed by R. Carlos Nakai. It requires learning one finger position for each note appearing on the staff. For example, the note on the first space of the staff is played by covering all six holes. This system works with any key flute that is properly tuned to the Native American Scale.

NOTE: To read Nakai Tablature you need to understand duration just as any musician does. It is not difficult and in this book I have presented all the information you will need to do so.

Duration Value: the length of time a musical tone sounds. You have learned the duration value of each of the following: *whole notes, quarter notes, half notes, eighth notes, dotted half notes, dotted quarter notes and sixteenth notes.*

Pentatonic scale: A five note scale also known as The Native American Scale.

You have completed lesson 5.

The Major Scale

Just as most traditional Native American melodies are played using the five notes of the Native American scale, most non-traditional songs are played using the seven notes of the Major scale. This includes Folk, Pop, Jazz and Classical themes.

Notes

You can play the major scale on your flute if you start on the second note from the bottom. You already know five of these notes because they are the same five notes you learned for the Native American Scale.

Fingering for the Major Scale:

Asterisks indicate "new" notes now introduced by the Major Scale

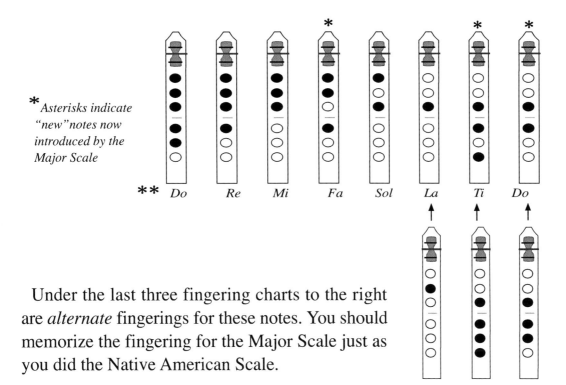

Do   Re   Mi   Fa   Sol   La   Ti   Do

Under the last three fingering charts to the right are *alternate* fingerings for these notes. You should memorize the fingering for the Major Scale just as you did the Native American Scale.

***Underneath the finger diagrams I have used 'Do Re Mi Fa Sol La Ti Do' because the sound of these well known tones is synonomous with the sound of the Major Scale and fit any Key flute you might have, even though the **actual pitch** of the notes will be different. Here is the sound of the Major Scale. Follow the illustration above as you listen.* Track 22

The following are exercises to help you learn to play the *Major Scale*. There are eight fingerings involved in playing these notes. If you have been doing your homework you already know five of them. If not, please go back to the Tablature exercises on pages 50 – 52 and learn them! If you like you may make a face at the teacher. *Practice two measures at a time and play each complete line three times.*

The Major Scale

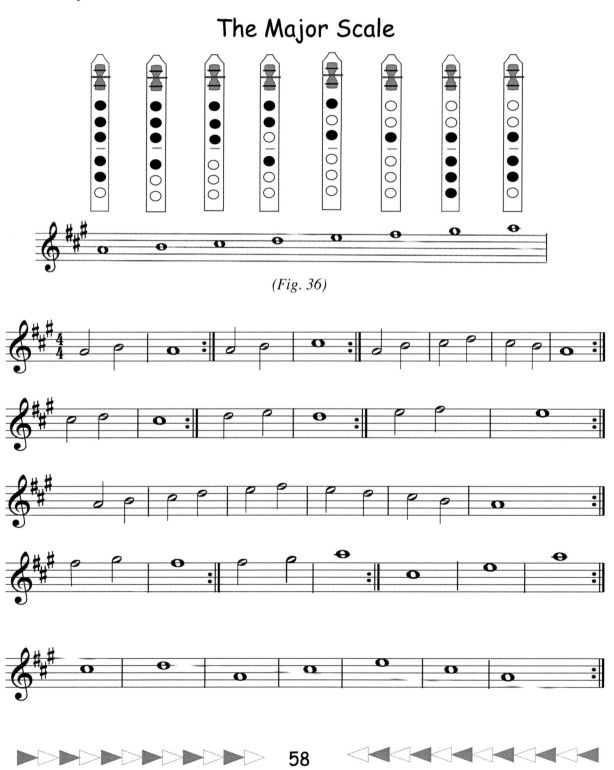

(Fig. 36)

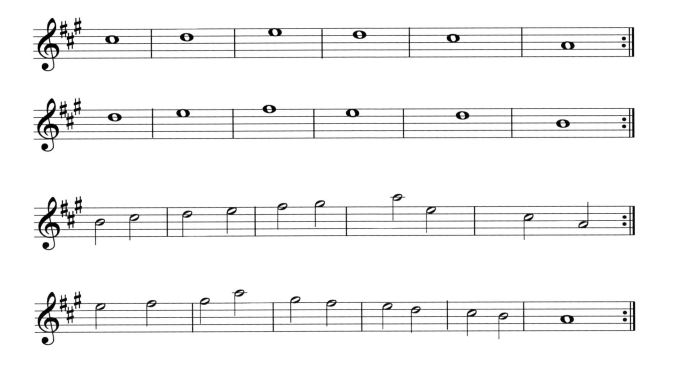

Now, test your reading skills on "Saints":

When the Saints Go Marching In

One more important concept in music notation is the *time signature:*

It appears as two numbers, one over the other at the beginning of a printed score. These are the three most common time signatures and what they tell you about the music you are about to play.

.

4	There are four beats in each measure.
4	The quarter note gets one beat.
3	There are three beats in each measure.
4	The quarter note gets one beat.
6	There are six beats in each measure.
8	The eighth note gets one beat.

Each of these time signatures gives the printed songs you will be playing in Part II a distinctive rhythmic feel.

* The mark (>) is an accent. It means stress or play the first note of each measure a little louder than the rest of the beats in the measure.

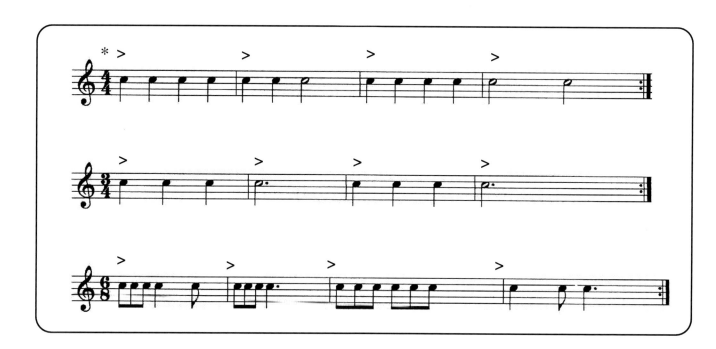

Final Review

Vibrato: The wave in the sound of the flute that gives it warmth and helps with emotional expression.

Major Scale: A seven note scale in which the pattern of whole and half steps is: whole, whole, half, whole, whole, whole, half. You can play the Major Scale on any flute if you start on the second note from the bottom. It is also called the diatonic scale.

Key Signature: The arrangement of sharps or flats at the beginning of a staff which indicates the tonality or key of the piece.

Time Signature: The 2 numbers at the beginning of a song: the top number tells how many beats in a measure. The bottom number tells what kind of note gets one beat.

Pitch: How high or how low a tone sounds. Finger diagrams for flute indicate pitch only. Notes placed on a staff indicate pitch and duration.

Treble Clef: The symbol (𝄞) which designates the second line of the staff as G above middle C. Also known as the G clef.

Accent: Emphasis given to certain tones. An accent sign appears as (>).

Congratulations! You have completed Part I

Welcome to Part II.

I know you will enjoy this new challenge. The following songs may be played on any key flute you may have as long as it is tuned to the pentatonic scale. I will be demonstrating them on an A minor which is the flute I have used on our lessons .

All the songs through *"Child's Play"* use the Native American Scale. Starting with *"Merrily We Roll Along"* we will use the Major Scale which is used most of the time for Pop, Folk, Jazz and Classical themes. The importance of playing these Folk tunes is that your ear becomes accustomed to the Key note drawing the other notes towards it. The key note is also called the tonic or fundamental.

SONGS

Take your songs from nature and you
will always have beautiful melodies

Lakota Courting Song

Traditional

Zuni Sunrise

Traditional

 *Track# 23*

Kiowa Love Song

Traditional

Track# 24

Sioux Chant

Traditional

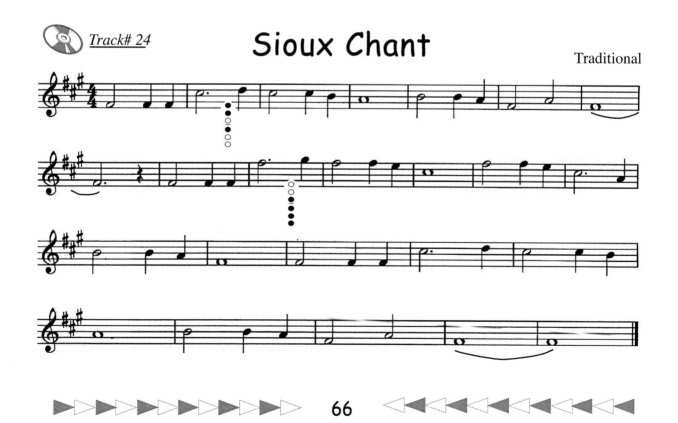

Track# 25

Medicine Song

Traditional

Track# 26

Lonesome Flute Song

Traditional

Prayer

John Vames

Koko's Lament

Track# 28

John Vames

Child's Play

 _Track# 29_

John Vames

Merrily We Roll Along

American

Love Somebody

American Folk

Lightly Row

American Folk

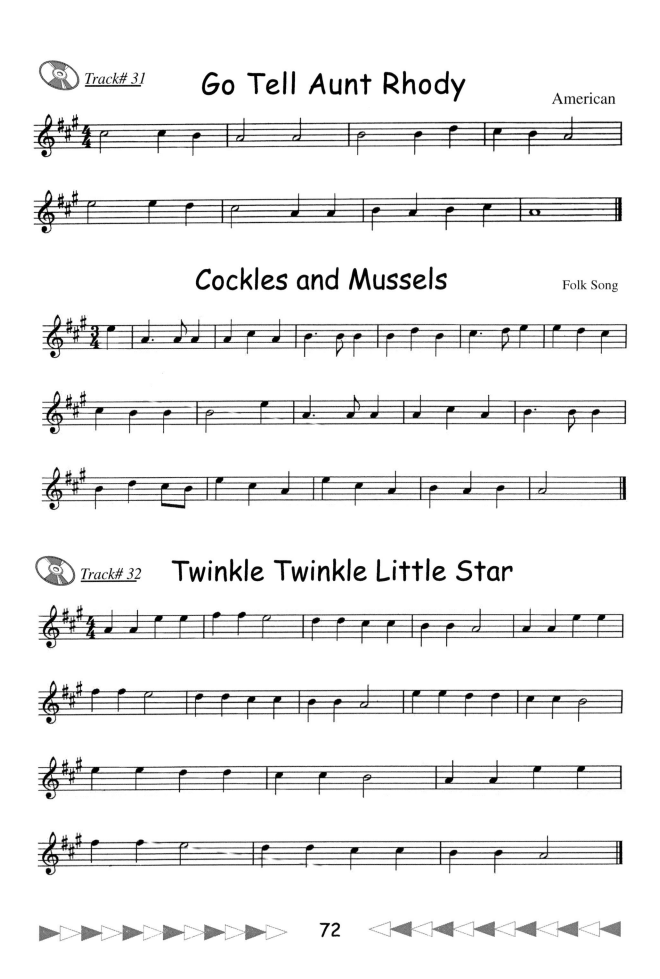

Blow The Man Down

Folk Song

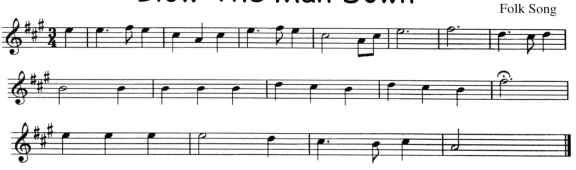

Oh How Lovely Is The Evening

English

Track# 33

Oh Susanna

Folk Song

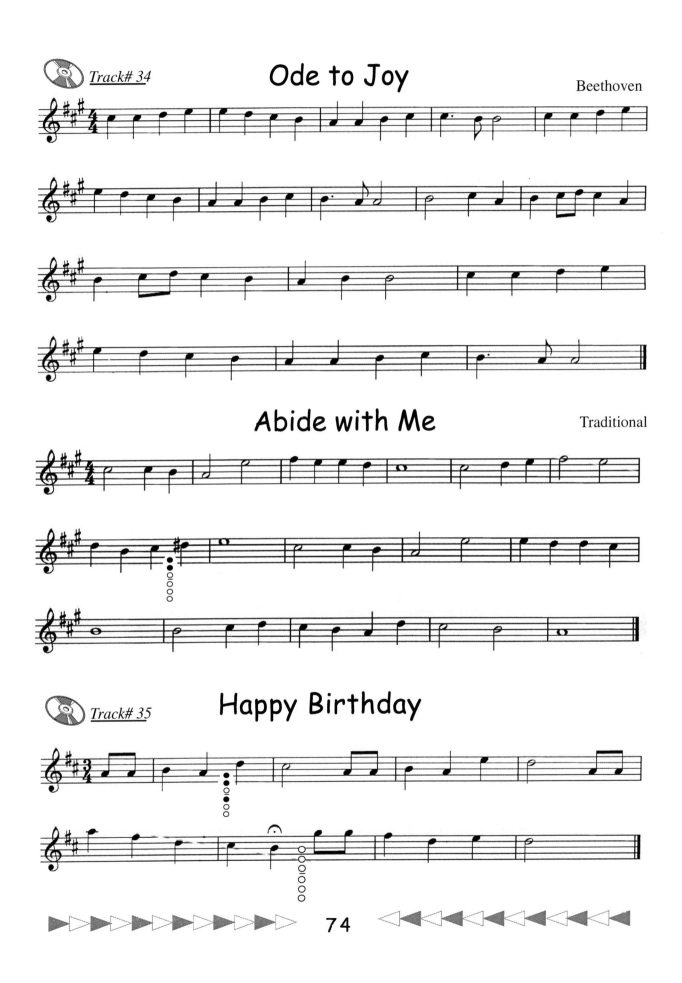

Track# 36 # Here Comes The Bride

Mendelsshon

* Notice that both of these songs have only two sharps in their key signature. F# and C#, They are both in the key of "D" Major

John Newton
J. Correll
D. Clayton

Track# 37 # Amazing Grace

Traditional Folk

This is in the key of B Major.
*All D's in this scale are D# as illustrated

Track# 38

Going Home

Antonin Dvorak

Track# 39

Blue Flute

John Vames

Appendix I

Useful Scales for Playing
Native American Flute:

Definition of a Scale:

1   A scale is a tonal ladder. A series of tones that can move from low to high or high to low.

2   The highest tone is one octave above the lowest tone. We call this interval (the distance between two tones) an Octave, from the Greek word meaning eight.

3   In our Music the number of tones between an octave varies from 5 to 7 notes.

4   The five note scale is called pentatonic because it contains five different tones. (Penta means "five" in Greek.)

5   The black keys on the piano make up a pentatonic scale and are the best aid to understanding the sound of this scale.

6   The eight note scale contains seven different notes and is called a diatonic scale.

Here are the Scales:

1 Native American Scale (Minor Pentatonic)
Mode 1

The most common scale used to play both traditional and contemporary songs. Brackets indicate alternate fingerings.

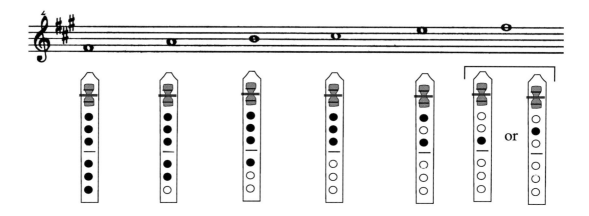

2 Minor Pentatonic
Mode 4

This next scale is useful for variety in playing songs with a Native American flavor. The second note above the fundamental (*) tends to attract the other tones and becomes a good tone for ending a song.

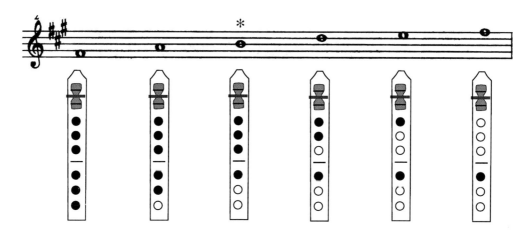

3 Major Pentatonic Scale

Yet another color to add to your musical palette. Called by some, the Chinese scale, the starting note is the tonic or key note.

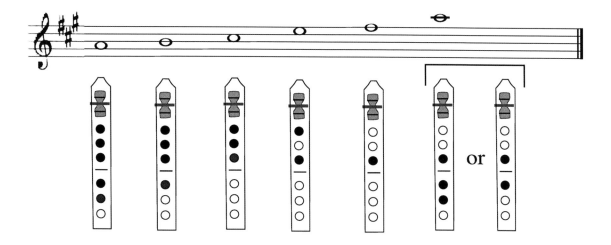

4 Relative Major Scale

The most common scale used in American and European music. Many folk songs, pop and jazz tunes as well as classical themes are based on this scale.

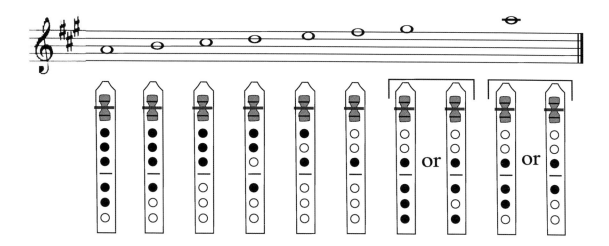

79

5 Chromatic Scale

This is actually a catalog of the fourteen useful notes playable on a well crafted six hole flute. By starting on the first note above the fundamental we can play a chromatic scale without using half holes.

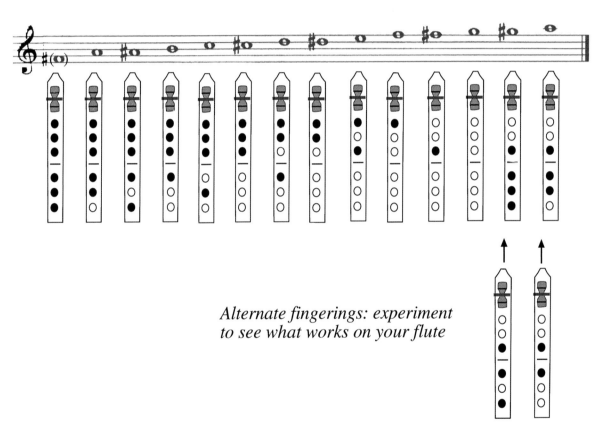

Alternate fingerings: experiment to see what works on your flute

Note: This scale is not used to make up melodies but rather as a reference to look up a note in a song that is unfamiliar to you.

Appendix II

Analysis of The Major Scale

To help you understand the nature of the Major Scale I have broken down the information you need into short statements. Each idea is numbered and clearly stated. Try to understand each statement before going on to the next. Take your time.

1. We use the first seven letters of the alphabet *A B C D E F G* to name the notes in our music system. When you reach "G" start with "A" again. Over and over…The lowest note on a full size piano keyboard is an "A and the sequence repeats over seven times.

2. On any key flute the scale will sound the same but the actual pitches and their specific names will be different.

3. The sequence of letters starting with "C" is the most important.

4. *C D E F G A B C* is the spelling for the C Major scale. Use a pencil and point to the keys in the following explanation:

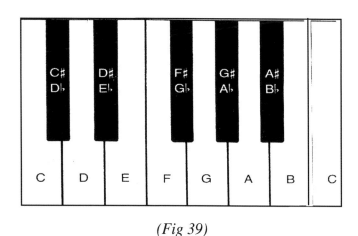

(Fig 39)

5. Notice the distance from E – F and B – C is smaller than the distance between C – D, D – E, F – G, G – A and A – B.

81

6. We call the distance between E – F and B – C a *half* step.

7. The distance between C – D, D - E , F – G, G – A, and A – B is called a *whole* step.

8. Notice that each of the black keys has two names. Example: the black key between C and D can be either C# or Db.

> *NOTE:* A sharp (#) tells us to move upward to the nearest key to the right. A flat (b) tells us to move downward to the nearest key to the left.

It is the pattern of whole steps and half steps that gives identity to a scale.

9. The pattern of whole and half steps for the major scale is *W W H W W W H.*

10. If we start a scale on "A" here is how it comes out: Study the diagram as you read the text.

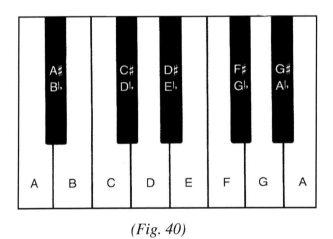

(Fig. 40)

A – B is a whole step. B – C is a half step. With reference to # 9 above, the pattern of whole and half steps for the major scale is: *w w h w w w h.* Therefore, *It should be a whole step so I raise it a half step and call it C#.*

C# – D is a half step as it should be. D – E is correct. E to F is a half step, *but again should be a whole step, so I raise the F a half step and call it F#.*

F# – G is a half step. *It should be a whole step so I raise it a half step and call it G#.* G# to A is correct.

11. Here are the notes of the "A" Major Scale placed on a staff with a sharp sign in front of each note that needs to be raised.

12. Instead of putting the sharp signs in front of these notes to identify them as being raised, we will abbreviate the procedure by taking the sharps and placing them on the staff after the Clef sign like this:

13. We call this grouping of sharps at the left side of the staff the *key signature*. It tells us that the notes, F , C, and G will be played sharp in the music that follows.

14. Most of the songs in this book are in A Major with the exception of *Amazing Grace*, *Happy Birthday* and *Here Comes The Bride*.

APPENDIX III

This is a catalog of rhythmic values you will encounter. It includes the illustrations of the symbols used to indicate both notes and rests

Rhythmic Values
(in 4/4 time)

Note	Name	Duration	Equivalent Rest
𝅝	Whole	4 beats	▬
𝅗𝅥.	Dotted half	3 beats	▬.
𝅗𝅥	Half	2 beats	▬
♩.	Dotted Qtr	1 1/1 beats	𝄽.
♩	Quarter	1 beat	𝄽
♪.	Dotted eighth	3⁄4 beat	𝄾.
♪	Eighth	1⁄2 beat	𝄾
♬	Sixteenth	1⁄4 beat	𝄿

APPENDIX IV

Caring For Your Flute

Your flute is almost maintenance free. Keep it in a cloth bag, a case made of PVC pipe or even a document mailer from an office supply store. Be careful not to expose it to extreme weather conditions (heat, cold, dampness) and it will give you a lifetime of enjoyment.

Be aware that sometimes after an extended period pf playing, condensation may form in the upper chamber. When this moisture gets into the narrow wind channel between the Fetish and the flute body you will not get a sound. Do not be concerned as this is what is known as "watering out". To rectify the situation grasp the flute from the lower end and shake it vigorously to release the moisture. You can also draw air back into your mouth like sipping through a straw. A third idea is to partially close off the "window" in front of the fetish to prevent any sound from coming out and then blow forcefully into the mouthpiece to expel any moisture.

Sometimes after a very long playing session when your flute does water out it is a good idea to untie and remove the Fetish and dry everything with a soft cloth. You can then lay the flute aside over night to air-dry completely.

Note: For most playing sessions lasting one hour or less none of the above will be necessary, and you will enjoy it as a maintenance free instrument.

Tip: The fetish must be kept tied tightly. Even so, it can be moved slightly back and Forth to find the "sweet spot" where it will play with a clear sound.

Glossary of Musical Terms

Accent: A stress or emphasis given to certain tones. An accent sign looks like this >

Accidental: A sign introduced before a note in a song that changes the pitch for one measure only. # (Sharp), b (flat), ♮ (natural).

Bar line: A vertical line through the staff to indicate a boundary for a measure of music.

Beat: The underlying steady pulse present in most music; the rhythmic unit to which one responds in marching or dancing.

Binary Form: A musical form made up of two sections, A and B, that contrast with each other.

Clef: A symbol placed on a staff to designate a precise pitch that identifies the other pitches in the music.

Compound meter: a grouping of beats (meter) in which the beat is divided into three equal parts.

Diatonic a seven-tone scale, consisting of five whole steps and two half steps, utilizing every pitch name. Major and minor scales are diatonic scales.

Drone: An accompaniment created by sounding one or more tones (usually two, five notes apart) simultaneously and continuously throughout a composition or section of a composition; a special type of harmony.

Duration: The length of time a musical tone sounds.

Folk Song: A song having no known composer, usually transmitted orally. And reflecting the musical consensus of a cultural group.

Form: The plan, order or design in which a piece of music is organized, incorporating repetition and contrast.

Grace Note: A short note printed in small type, that ornaments the note that follows it. A grace note is crushed into the main note and has no time value.

Half step: The smallest interval in our music. B - C and E - F on the piano keyboard are half steps.

Improvisation: Music performed extemporaneously. Often within a framework determined by the musical style being used.

Major Scale: A scale in which the pattern of whole and half steps is: whole, whole, half, whole, whole, whole, half.

Measure: A unit of beats determined by bar lines; informally called a "bar".

Glossary of Musical Terms

Melody: A succession of sounds (pitches) and silences moving one at a time through time.

Modes: Scales (each with seven notes) consisting of various patterns of whole and half steps. The seven possible modes – Ionian, Dorian, Phrygian, Lydian, Mixolydian, Aeolian, and Locrian – were used in the medieval and Renenaissance periods and served as the basis from which major and minor scales emerged.

Motive: A brief rhythmic or melodic figure that recurs throughout a composition as a unifying element.

Natural: A sign that cancels a sharp or a flat: A note that is neither sharp nor flat, as C, D, E, F, G, and A, B on the piano keyboard. (♮)

Octave: The interval in which two pitches share the same letter name (C-C) and are eight steps apart (eight lines and spaces from one note to the next); one pitch with twice the frequency of the other.

Pentatonic Scale: A five-tone scale often identified with the pattern of the black keys of the piano.

Phrase: A musical segment with a clear beginning and ending, comparable to a simple sentence or a clause in speech.

Rhythm: All of the duration or lengths of sounds and silences that occur in music; the organization of sounds and silences in time.

Scale: A pattern of pitches arranged in ascending or descending order. Scales are identified by their specific arrangement of whole and half steps.

Sharp: A symbol that raises the pitch a half step (#).

Theme: A distinctive melodic statement, usually part of a long movement.

Tie: A curved line that connects two identical pitches and indicates that they should be performed as a single note; to perform, play the first note only and hold through the time value of the second. (⌒)

Time Signature: The two numbers at the beginning of a song 4/4 3/4 6/8. The top number tells how many beats in a measure. The bottom number tells what kind of note gets one beat.

Tonality: The relationship of tones in a scale to the tonic.

Tonal Music: Music that is centered on a particular tonic or key center.

Tonic: The central tone or chord of the key and the first note or chord of a major or minor scale.

Treble Clef: The symbol (𝄞) which designates the second line of the staff as G above middle C.

Triplet: When 3 notes are grouped together with a figure "3" above or below the notes, the group is called a *triplet*. The three notes of a triplet group are equal to one quarter note.

Whole Step: An interval that comprises two consecutive half steps, as C to D. (C to C# is a half step).

Closing Notes

I hope you have enjoyed these lessons as much as I have enjoyed preparing them for you. There will always be more challenges but rest assured, with the hardest one behind you now the best is yet to come. If you have come this far you have acquired all the right tools to continue on whatever path you choose. It is your journey that lies ahead: your songs to be played. You might recall the same feeling of excitement when you first received your driver's license. My advice to you is take to the road and play on!

I know you will find your flute to be a faithful companion, there when you need one the most. So many times I have arrived home at the end of a day, exhausted by the stresses of our civilized world. There waits one of my friends, needing to be played as much as I need to play it. And so I play, and soon I feel well again, relaxed, renewed and satisfied. I wish the same for you.

There is a wealth of information you can find about the powers of this instrument. I am also certain that you will hear many a "flute story" that testifies to it. Perhaps one day you will tell your own: how learning to play the Native American Flute changed your life. My own flute story led me to a reality I had not imagined. The thought of writing this book was as far from my conscious mind as the idea of living in Timbuktu. Nevertheless though, here it is and I might add, my second book, *"Song For Koko: Jazz for Native American Flute"* is now available. If you would like a copy, please visit my website at www.flutejourneyworkshops.com or call 888-884-9604. "Song for Koko" is an excellent tool for traveling further on your journey.

In closing I wish to say that "Understanding the Gift" was written to enable anyone with a song in their heart to release that song and realize the healing power of music.

May you walk in beauty and enjoy this gift...

About the Author

John Vames has been playing and teaching music for the last 30 years. The focus of his teaching is not only to develop professional Musicians but also to show students how to create and enjoy music for the enrichment of their own lives. With his help hundreds of people of all ages have learned to play clarinet, sax, transverse flute, Native American Flute and Classical and Jazz piano.

As a graduate of Northwestern University with a Masters Degree in Music theory, John spent his undergraduate years at the University of Chicago in the days of Robert Maynard Hutchins and Mortimer Adler. Like his predecessors his greatest love was the humanities. Music especially has been a life long pursuit....

In the summer of 1995 while vacationing in Santa Fe, he first became acquainted with the sound of the Native American Flute. As an educator, he realized how easy it was for almost anyone to play. Unlike piano or guitar that take years of study, this instrument could be mastered in a short time. What has followed since is his initiation of Native American Flute Classes at *Scottsdale Community College* in Scottsdale, Arizona, including a one semester course for credit.

Also currently underway in Phoenix and surrounding areas at numerous times throughout the year are *Beginning, Intermediate, and Advanced Workshops* in special half-day presentations. John is available for guest appearances, performance/demonstrations, workshops, special functions and Wellness Retreats.

For further information please contact www.flutejourneyworkshops.com

More By John Vames

 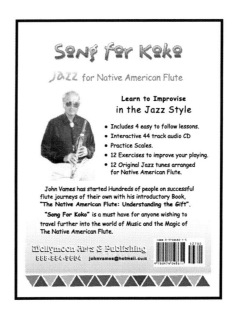

Jazz has its own language. In "Song For Koko", jazz rhythm, tempo, and form are explained and demonstrated in written studies and on the accompanying CD. Also included are 12 Original Jazz Tunes arranged for Native American Flute. This book is a must have for anyone wishing to travel further into the world of music and the magic of the flute.

Prerequisites: reading written music for Native American Flute and the ability to improvise melodies in the Native American style.

ORDER LINE: 888-884-9604 Visa/MC/AX

Checks: Molly Moon Arts & Publishing
8513 East Mulberry Street
Scottsdale, Arizona 85251

PayPal: mollymoonarts@hotmail.com

Resources

Ball, Jeff. *Trailhead of the American Indian Courting Flute.* Red Feather Music, Boulder, Co. 1994

Burton, Bryan. *Voices of the Wind,* World Music Press 1998

Bludts, Carl. *The Four Directions*, Rabbitdog Publishing 1999

Crawford, Tim R. and Kathleen Joyce-Grendahl, Editor. *Flute Magic: An Introduction to the Native American Flute* (Second Edition). 1999

Edgar, Bob. *The Native American Flute Book – How to Play the Flute and Spirit Songs.* Rabbits' Run Press. Santa Cruz, Ca. 1995

Goble, Paul. *Love Flute*, Bradbury Press, New York, NY 1986

Nakai, R. Carlos and James DeMars. *The Art of the Native American Flute.* Canyon Records Productions. Phoenix, Az. 1996

Perkins, Laura Lee, *The Native American Flute Tutor,* White Owl Creations, Seaport Me., 2000

Shanet, Howard. *Learn To Read Music*, A Fireside Book published by Simon & Shuster Inc. 1956

Owusu, Heike. *Symbols of Native America*, Sterling Publishing, New York 1997

Paxton Price, Lew. *Creating and Using the Native American Love Flute*, 2nd Edition, El Dorado Press 1993 and 1994

SUBJECT INDEX